For Annie with love – M.R.
For Isobel with love – B.C.

Text copyright © 2001 Margaret Ryan
Illustrations copyright © 2001 Ben Cort

Published in Great Britain in 2001
by Hodder Wayland, an imprint of
Hodder Children's Books

British Library Cataloguing in Publication Data
Ryan, Margaret, 1944 -
Tidy Up, Harry!
1. Harry (Fictitious character) – Juvenile fiction 2. Autumn
- Juvenile fiction 3. Children's stories
I. Title
823.9'14 [J]

ISBN: 0 7502 3610 8

Printed in Hong Kong by Wing King Tong Co. Ltd.

Hodder Children's Books
A division of Hodder Headline Limited
338 Euston Road, London NW1 3BH

MARGARET RYAN

Tidy Up, Harry!

Illustrated by Ben Cort

HODDER
Wayland

an imprint of Hodder Children's Books

Harry was helping his dad tidy up the
garden.
"Pick up the fallen apples, Harry," said
his dad, "and put them into a
cardboard box."

5

"Okay," said Harry.
He went round and round the big
apple tree picking up the fallen apples.

There were lots of them, hiding under
the crispy brown leaves.

When the cardboard box was full,
Harry picked it up.

WHUMP! The bottom fell out of the box and the apples rolled all over the garden.

8

"Oh, no," said Harry. "Now I'll have to pick up the apples all over again. This is hard work. I don't like Autumn."

He had just finished loading the apples
into his old go-cart when his dad said . . .
"Pick up the prickly branches, Harry,
and put them into the wheelbarrow."

"Oh, all right," said Harry.
He went round and round the garden
picking up the prickly branches. There
were lots of them, lying under the shrubs.

When the wheelbarrow was full, Harry
picked up the handles.

WHOOPS! Next door's dog ran into the garden and knocked over Harry and the wheelbarrow. The branches were scattered all over the garden.

"Oh, no," said Harry. "Now I'll have
to pick up the branches all over again.
This is hard work. I really don't like
Autumn."

14

He had just finished picking up the
branches when his dad said . . .
"Take this brush, Harry, and sweep up
the crispy brown leaves into a neat pile."

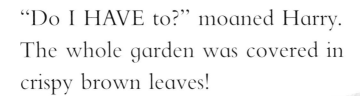

"Do I HAVE to?" moaned Harry. The whole garden was covered in crispy brown leaves!

Harry took the brush and began to
sweep up the leaves.
He had just finished when a big wind
sprang up. WHEEEEEEE! The leaves
whirled all over the garden again.

"Oh, no," cried Harry. "Now I'll have to chase the leaves as well as sweep them up. This is hard work. I really really don't like Autumn."

He had just finished sweeping up the leaves when his dad said . . .

"There's one more thing you can help me with, Harry."

"Oh, no," cried Harry. "Not more roly poly apples. Not more prickly branches. Not more whirling leaves. Not more hard work. I really really don't like Autumn at all!"

His dad smiled. "I think you might like this. I want you to help me make a bonfire with all the leaves and branches."

"Make a bonfire!" cried Harry. "Why didn't you tell me before? I love bonfires!"

22

Harry helped his dad pile up all the leaves and branches, then watched as his dad lit the fire.

Red and yellow flames licked up through the bonfire and made a crickly crackly noise.

Harry laughed and danced round
and round.

"Can I go and look for more leaves and branches to put on the bonfire?" he said. "This is great fun."

"I thought you said it was hard work,"
smiled his dad.

"I've been working hard too," said
Harry's mum, coming out of the house.
"Look what I've made with your
apples, Harry."

And she handed him a large, sticky, toffee apple. "This is for helping Dad to tidy up."

"Thank you," grinned Harry. He stuck out his tongue and gave the apple an enormous lick.

"This is my favourite kind of work," he said. "I really love Autumn."

Follow Harry through all four seasons, in these exciting Bright Stars Books:

Harry and the Tiger by Margaret Ryan

It's Spring time, and Harry and his class are going on an exciting visit to a farm! They'll meet lambs, ducklings and piglets. But what Harry really wants to see is a tiger. Silly Harry! You don't get tigers on farms . . . do you?

Harry Keeps His Cool by Margaret Ryan

It's Summer time, and Harry's feeling hot hot hot! He's in the garden with his family, finding ways to have fun. Now he's got hold of the garden hose . . . Oh no! Don't do that, Harry!

Harry's Footprints by Margaret Ryan

It's Winter time, and Harry wants to be the first to stamp his footprints in the snow. But can he put on his gloves, anorak and boots before the rest of the family get out there too?

All these Bright Stars can be purchased from your local bookseller. For more information about Bright Stars, write to:
The Sales Department,
Hodder Children's Books,
A division of Hodder Headline Limited,
338 Euston Road,
London NW1 3BH